Special thanks to Rabbi Mark Cooper
for his careful review of the text.

Published in the United States 2007 by
🍎 Blue Apple Books
P.O. Box 1380, Maplewood, N.J. 07040
www.blueapplebooks.com

Distributed in the U.S. by Chronicle Books
First Edition
Printed in China

ISBN 13 : 978-1-59354-600-7
ISBN 10 : 1-59354-600-9

1 3 5 7 9 10 8 6 4 2

JOSH HANFT

THE MIRACLES OF PASSOVER

ILLUSTRATED BY
SEYMOUR CHWAST

BLUE APPLE BOOKS

For many years, the Jews in Egypt peacefully lived side by side with their Egyptian neighbors.

But then a new Pharaoh came to power in Egypt, and he treated the Jews harshly. The Pharaoh was afraid that the Jews would rise up against him, so he forced the Jews to become his slaves. Cruel taskmasters punished the Jews when they could not finish their many tasks.

But even after making the Jews his slaves, the Pharaoh was so afraid of them that he sent out an order for all Jewish baby boys to be drowned.

One mother refused to obey this order. She placed her baby in a basket and floated the basket down the river. She hoped that someone would find the baby and take care of him.

Someone did find the baby—the Pharaoh's daughter. She took pity on the baby and brought him up in Pharaoh's palace. She named him Moses, which means "I drew him out of the water."

Even though Moses grew up in the palace, he never forgot the difficult life of his people. One day he saw a slave driver beat a Jewish man, and he became so angry that he killed the slave driver. Afraid that he would be punished, Moses ran away and worked as a shepherd.

While tending his flock one day, Moses saw a burning bush in the desert.

Moses returned to Egypt and
went before the Pharaoh.
"Let my people go!" he cried.
But the Pharaoh refused to free
the Jews, and instead made their
lives even harder.

Moses asked G-d for help.
G-d told Moses to go back and
warn the Pharaoh that if he did
not free the Jews, the Egyptians
would suffer from plagues.

When Moses told the Pharaoh about G-d's warning, Pharaoh didn't believe him. As a sign of G-d's power, Moses threw down his staff. Right before the Pharaoh's eyes it turned into a wriggling snake.

Pharaoh's magician also turned his staff into a snake.

Moses went back to the Pharaoh and asked him again and again to free the Jews. But the Pharaoh remained unmoved. Each time he refused, G-d sent a new plague to the Egyptian people.

With each plague, the Pharaoh promised to let the Jews go. But as soon as each plague ended, the Pharaoh broke his promise.

At last, G-d sent the final plague to Egypt: the firstborn of each Egyptian family would be killed. To protect the Jews from this terrible plague, G-d told them to paint their doorways with the blood of a lamb to show that they were His people. G-d would pass over the houses of His people, and their children would live.

Finally, the Pharaoh agreed to let the Jews go.
Moses gathered the Jews together and led them
out of Egypt under the cover of night.

But the Pharaoh still could not bear to lose his slaves,

so he sent his soldiers after them.

When the Jews reached the Red Sea,
they stopped at the water's edge,
unable to cross. The Pharaoh's
soldiers were right behind them.

But Moses held his staff
over the Red Sea . . .

and the waters parted,
allowing the Jews to cross safely.

The soldiers followed closely behind. But when the Jews reached the other side, the sea closed back up on the soldiers, and they all perished beneath the waves.

Ever since, wherever they have lived, Jews have celebrated the miracle of having been saved with a Passover *seder*.

During the seder, they read from a *Haggadah*. This book retells the story of the Jews' exodus, or departure, out of Egypt.

At the seder, special foods are eaten.
Each food in the Passover meal is meant
to remind us of the Passover story.

WINE

KARPAS

LAMB SHANK

EGG

BITTER HERBS

HAROSET

MATZA

A piece of matza is broken off and hidden during the seder.
After the meal, children look for this piece, called the *afikoman*.
It is the last food eaten at a seder.

At the end of the seder we open the door for Elijah to join
the seder and drink his cup of wine.

We wait for the time when Elijah will announce the days of peace for everyone.

We end the seder with these words:

"NEXT YEAR IN JERUSALEM!"